BEDTIME

STORIES *and* RHYMES

Selected by
Alistair Hedley

Illustrated by
Kate Aldous, Sue Clarke, Claire Henley,
Anna Cynthia Leplar, Jacqueline Mair,
Sheila Moxley, Karen Perrins,
Jane Tattersfield and Sara Walker

p

Contents

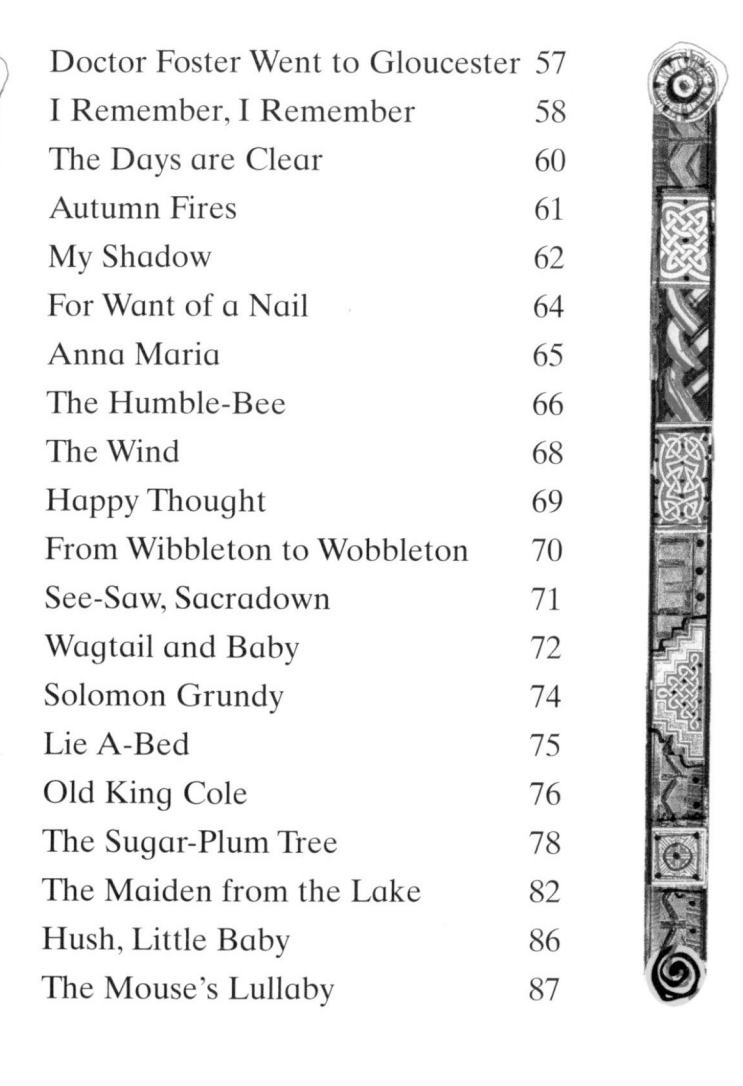

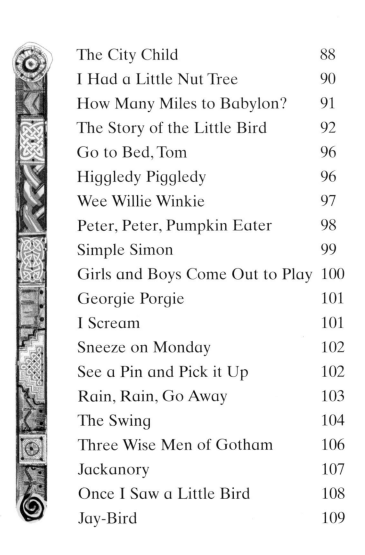

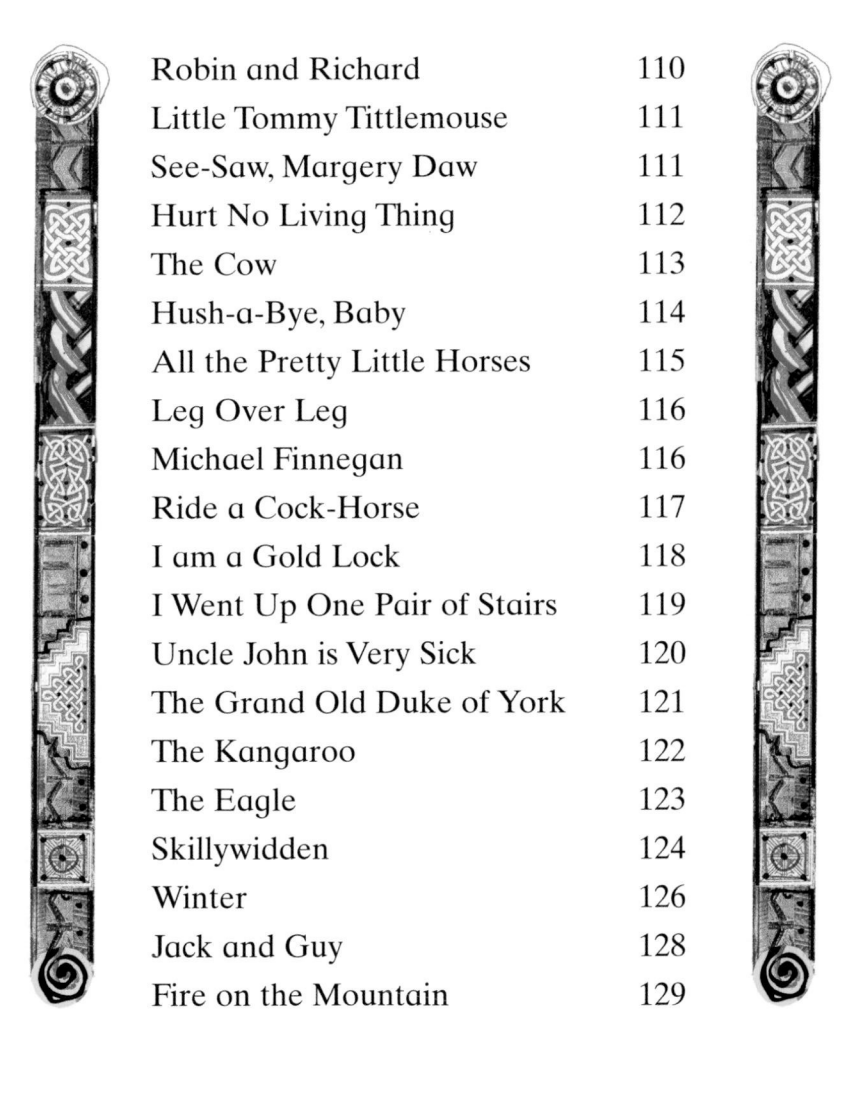

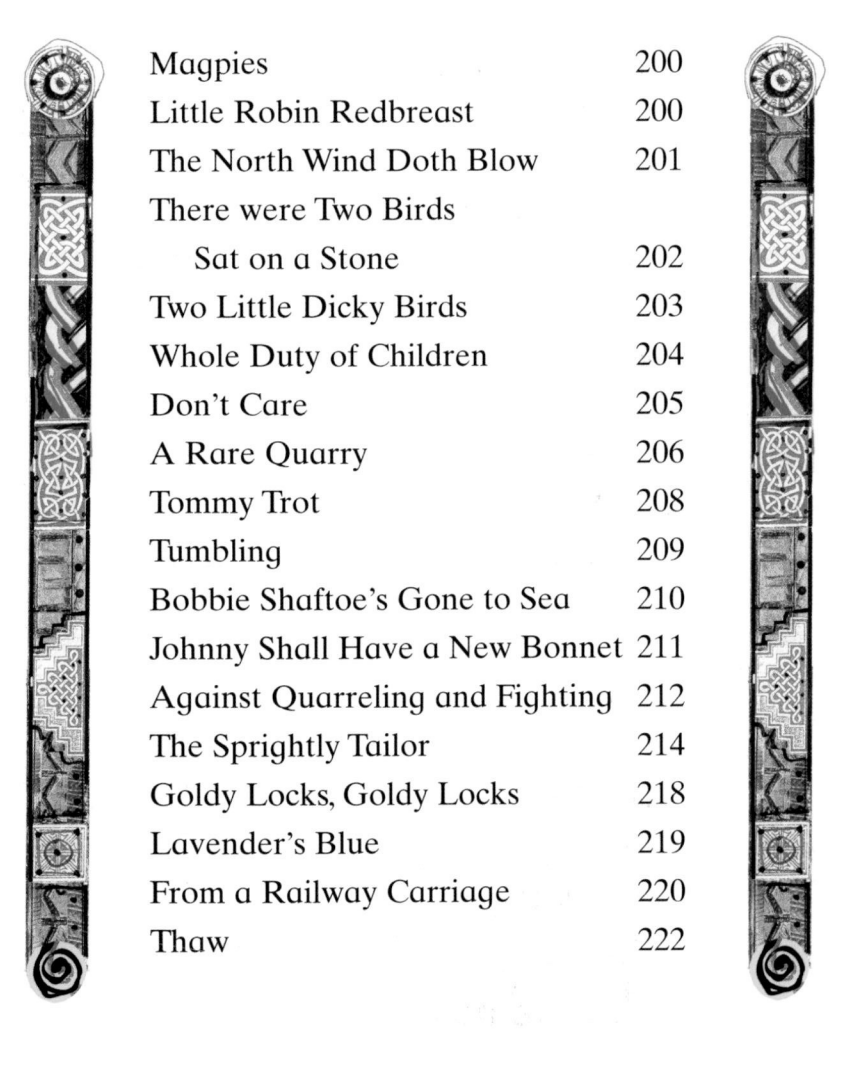

ANNA BANANA

Anna Banana
Played the piano;
The piano broke
And Anna choked.

LUCY LOCKET

Lucy Locket lost her pocket,
  Kitty Fisher found it,
But not a penny was there in it,
  Just the binding round it.

LITTLE MISS MUFFET

Little Miss Muffet
Sat on a tuffet,
Eating her curds and whey;
There came a great spider,
Who sat down beside her,
And frightened Miss Muffet away.

BAA, BAA, BLACK SHEEP

Baa, baa, black sheep, have you any wool?
Yes, sir, yes, sir, three bags full;
One for the master, one for the dame,
And one for the little boy that lives
   down the lane.

MARY HAD A LITTLE LAMB

Mary had a little lamb,
Its fleece was white as snow,
And everywhere that Mary went
The lamb was sure to go.

It followed her to school one day,
Which was against the rule;
It made the children laugh and play
To see a lamb in school.

THE MILLER OF DEE

There was a jolly miller
  Lived on the river Dee,
He worked and sung from morn till night,
  No lark so blithe as he;
And this the burden of his song
  For ever used to be—
I jump mejerrime jee!
  I care for nobody—no! not I,
Since nobody cares for me.

AS I WAS GOING ALONG

As I was going along, long, long,
A-singing a comical song, song, song,
The lane that I went was so long,
long, long,
And the song that I sung was as long,
long, long,
And so I went singing along.

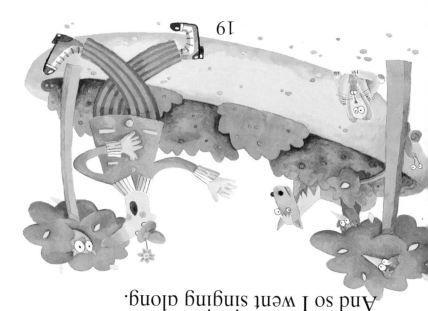

TO MARKET, TO MARKET

To market, to market,
To buy a plum bun;
Home again, come again,
Market is done.

THIS LITTLE PIGGY

This little piggy went to market,
This little piggy stayed at home,
This little piggy had roast beef,
This little piggy had none,
And this little piggy cried, *Wee-wee-wee*,
 All the way home.

THERE WAS AN OLD WOMAN
WHO LIVED IN A SHOE

There was an old woman who lived in a shoe,
She had so many children she didn't know
  what to do;
She gave them some broth without any bread;
And scolded them soundly and put them
  to bed.

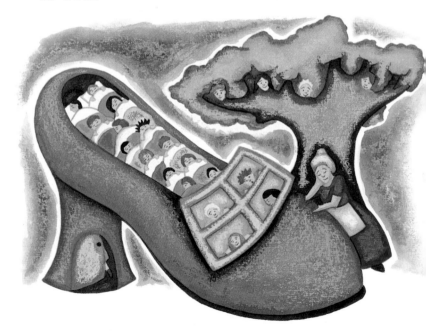

THERE WAS AN OLD WOMAN, AND WHAT DO YOU THINK?

There was an old woman, and what do
  you think?
She lived upon nothing but victuals
  and drink.
Victuals and drink were the chief of
  her diet;
This tiresome old woman could
  never be quiet.

23

JACK SPRAT

Jack Sprat would eat no fat,
His wife would eat no lean,
And so between the two of them
They licked the platter clean.

MINNIE AND MATTIE

Minnie and Mattie
  And fat little May,
Out in the country,
  Spending a day.

Such a bright day,
  With the sun glowing,
And the trees half in leaf,
  And the grass growing.

Pinky white pigling
  Squeals through his snout,
Woolly white lambkin
  Frisks all about.

Cluck! cluck! the nursing hen
  Summons her folk—
Ducklings all downy soft,
  Yellow as yolk.

Cluck! cluck! the mother hen
  Summons her chickens
To peck the dainty bits
  Found in her pickings.

Minnie and Mattie
  And May carry posies,
Half of sweet violets,
  Half of primroses.

Give the sun time enough,
  Glowing and glowing,
He'll rouse the roses
  And bring them blowing.

Don't wait for roses
  Losing today,
O Minnie, Mattie,
  And wise little May.

Violets and primroses
  Blossom today
For Minnie and Mattie
  And fat little May.

CHRISTINA ROSSETTI

THE FROG

A widow asked her daughter to fetch some water from the well. When the daughter came to the well she found that it was dry. She wondered how they would manage without water, as it was high summer and there had been no rain for days. The poor girl was so anxious that she sat down by the well and began to cry.

Suddenly the girl heard a plop, and a frog jumped out of the well.

"Why are you crying?" asked the frog.

The girl explained to the little frog.

"Well," he said, "if you will be my wife, you shall have all the water you need."

The girl thought he was joking, and agreed to be his wife. When she pulled her bucket up again, it was full of water.

That evening, as she and her mother were going to bed, they heard a voice and a scratching sound at the door of their cottage: "Open the door. Remember the promise you made to me at the well."

"Ugh, it's a filthy frog," said the girl.

"Open the door to the poor creature," said her mother, for she was a kind woman. And so they opened the door.

"Give me my supper, my own true love. Remember the promise you made to me, when you fetched your water down at the well," the frog went on.

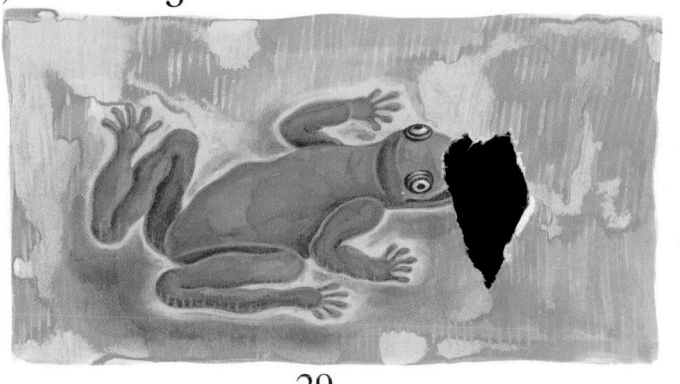

Reluctantly, the girl gave hir some supper.

"Put me to bed, my own true love. Remember the promise you made down at the well," said the frog.

"We can't have a slimy frog in our bed!" cried the daughte

"Put the creature to bed and let it rest," said the mother. So they turned down the sheets and the frog climbed into bed.

The frog spoke again: "Bring me an ax, my own true love. Remember the promise you made down at the well."

The widow and her daughter were puzzled. " an ax?" asked the girl.

"We shall d out why soon enough,"said the mother We will bring him an ax."

30

THE FROG

So they fetched an ax.
"Now chop off my head, my
wn true love. Remember
ie promise you made down
t the well," croaked the frog
) the daughter.
Trembling, the girl raised the
x high, and brought it down on
) the frog's neck. The girl looked away for
 moment, scared to see the creature and its
evered head. But, when she heard her
iother's shout of surprise, she looked—and
iere stood the finest, most handsome
oung prince that they had ever seen.
"It was me you promised to marry," smiled
ie prince. And the poor widow's daughter
nd the handsome prince *did* marry, and they
ved in happiness for the rest of their lives.

31

A THORN

I went to the wood and got it;
I sat me down and looked at it;
The more I looked at it the less I liked it;
And I brought it home because
  I couldn't help it.

TEETH

Thirty white horses upon a red hill,
Now they tramp, now they champ,
  now they stand still.

A STAR

I have a little sister, they call her Peep, Peep;
She wades the waters deep, deep, deep;
She climbs the mountains high, high, high;
Poor little creature, she has but one eye.

OVER THE HILLS AND FAR AWAY

When I was young and had no sense
I bought a fiddle for eighteen pence,
And the only tune that I could play
Was *Over the Hills and Far Away*.

HEY, DIDDLE, DIDDLE

Hey, diddle, diddle, the cat and the fiddle,
  The cow jumped over the moon;
The little dog laughed to see such sport,
  And the dish ran away with the spoon!

POLLY, PUT THE KETTLE ON

Polly, put the kettle on,
Polly, put the kettle on,
Polly, put the kettle on,
  We'll all have tea.

Sukey, take it off again,
Sukey, take it off again,
Sukey, take it off again,
  They've all gone away.

A PRETTY LITTLE GIRL

A pretty little girl in a round-eared cap
I met in the streets the other day;
  She gave me such a thump,
  That my heart it went bump,
I thought I should have fainted away!
I thought I should have fainted away!

A SWARM OF BEES IN MAY

A swarm of bees in May
Is worth a load of hay;
A swarm of bees in June
Is worth a silver spoon;
A swarm of bees in July
Is not worth a fly.

ITSY BITSY SPIDER

Itsy Bitsy Spider
  Climbing up the spout;
Down came the rain
  And washed the spider out.
Out came the sunshine
  And dried up all the rain;
Itsy Bitsy Spider
  Climbing up again.

OLIVER TWIST

Oliver Twist
You can't do this,
So what's the use
Of trying?
Touch your toe,
Touch your knee,
Clap your hands,
Away we go.

A SAILOR WENT TO SEA

A sailor went to sea, sea, sea,
To see what he could see, see, see,
But all that he could see, see, see,
Was the bottom of the deep blue
  sea, sea, sea.

THE MISSING KETTLE

A woman who lived on Sanntraigh, an island, had only a kettle to hang over the fire to boil water and cook food. Every day a fairy crept into the house to take the kettle

When this happened, the kettle handle clanked and the woman recited this rhyme:

A smith is able to make
Cold iron hot with coal.
The due of a kettle is bones,
And to bring it back again whole.

Then the fairy flew off with the kettle and brought it back later, full of meat and bone

One day the woman had to go on the ferry across to the mainland. She asked her husband to say the rhyme when the fairy came for the kettle. Her husband agreed and went back to work.

When he saw the fairy outside, the husband was afraid because he had had no contact with the little people. 'If I lock the cottage door,' he thought, 'he will go away and leave the kettle, and it will be just as if she had never come.' So the husband locked the door and did not open it. But the fairy flew up to the hole in the roof above the fire, and before the husband knew what was happening, the creature made the kettle jump up, straight out of the hole.

43

When his wife returned that evening, there was no kettle to be seen.

"Where is my kettle?" asked the woman.

"I don't know," said the husband. "I took fright and closed the door to the fairy. She took the kettle through the roof."

"You pathetic wretch! Can't you even mind the kettle when I go out for the day?"

Off went the woman to where the fairies lived, to see if she could get the kettle back.

There was only an old fairy sitting in the corner of the fairy knoll, so she thought that the others were out at their nightly mischief. She found her kettle, and noticed some fairy food still in it.

Picking up the kettle, she ran back down the lane with the sound of dogs chasing her. She took out some of the food from the

kettle, threw it to the dogs, and hurried on.
When the dogs began to catch her up, she
threw down more food. Finally, when she
got near her own gate, she poured out the
rest of the food, hoping that the dogs
would not come into her own house. Then
she ran inside and closed the door.

Every day after that the woman watched
for the fairy coming to take her kettle. But
the little creature never came again.

IF ALL THE WORLD WAS APPLE-PIE

If all the world was apple-pie,
  And all the sea was ink,
And all the trees were bread and cheese,
  What should we have for drink?

I EAT MY PEAS WITH HONEY

I eat my peas with honey,
I've done it all my life,
It makes the peas taste funny,
But it keeps them on my knife.

ANONYMOUS
AMERICAN

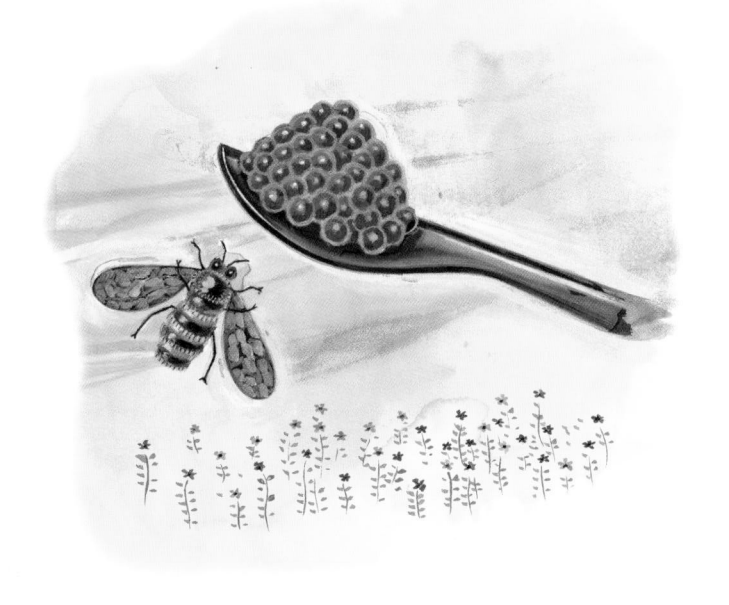

LADY MOON

Lady Moon, Lady Moon, where are
  you roving?
    Over the sea.
Lady Moon, Lady Moon, whom are
  you loving?
    All that love me.

Are you not tired with rolling, and never
  Resting to sleep?
Why look so pale, and so sad, as for ever
  Wishing to weep?

Ask me not this, little child, if you love me;
    You are too bold;
I must obey my dear Father above me,
    And do as I'm told.

Lady Moon, Lady Moon, where are
   you roving?
    Over the sea.
Lady Moon, Lady Moon, whom are
   you loving?
    All that love me.

RICHARD MONCKTON MILNES, LORD HOUGHTON

THE MOON

The moon has a face like the
    clock in the hall;
She shines on thieves on the
    garden wall,
On streets and fields and
    harbor quays,
And birdies asleep in the forks
    of the trees.

The squalling cat and the
squeaking mouse,
The howling dog by the door of
the house,
The bat that lies in bed at noon,
All love to be out by the light of
the moon.

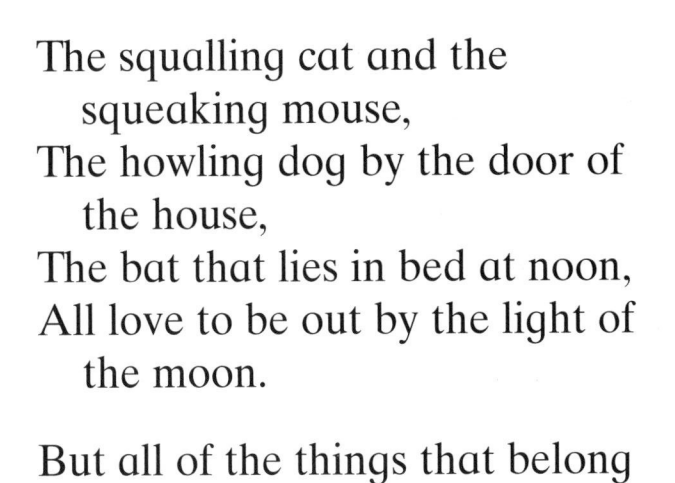

But all of the things that belong
to the day,
Cuddle to sleep to be out of her way;
And flowers and children close their eyes
Till up in the morning the sun
shall arise.

ROBERT LOUIS STEVENSON

HUMPTY DUMPTY

Humpty Dumpty sat on a wall,
Humpty Dumpty had a great fall;
All the king's horses and all the king's men
Couldn't put Humpty together again.

TWEEDLE-DUM AND TWEEDLE-DEE

Tweedle-dum and Tweedle-dee
  Agreed to have a battle,
For Tweedle-dum said Tweedle-dee
  Had spoiled his nice new rattle.
Just then flew down a monstrous crow,
  As big as a tar-barrel,
Which frightened both the heroes so,
  They quite forgot their quarrel.

MY GRANDMOTHER SENT ME

My grandmother sent me a new-fashioned three cornered cambric country cut handkerchief.

Not an old-fashioned three cornered cambric country cut handkerchief, but a new-fashioned three cornered cambric country cut handkerchief.

SWAN SWAM OVER THE SEA

Swan swam over the sea—
Swim, swan, swim,
Swan swam back again,
Well swum swan.

HEY, DOROLOT, DOROLOT!

Hey, dorolot, dorolot!
Hey, dorolay, dorolay!
Hey, my bonny boat, bonny boat,
Hey, drag away, drag away!

RUB-A-DUB DUB

Rub-a-dub dub,
Three men in a tub,
And who do you think they be?
The butcher, the baker,
The candle-stick maker,
And they all jumped out of a rotten potato

DOCTOR FOSTER WENT TO GLOUCESTER

Doctor Foster went to Gloucester,
  In a shower of rain;
He stepped in a puddle, up to his middle,
  And never went there again.

I REMEMBER, I REMEMBER

I remember, I remember
The house where I was born,
The little window where the sun
Came peeping in at morn;
He never came a wink too soon
Nor brought too long a day;
But now, I often wish the night
Had borne my breath away.

I remember, I remember
The roses, red and white,
The violets, and the lily-cups—
Those flowers made of light!
The lilacs where the robin built,
And where my brother set
The laburnum on his birthday—
The tree is living yet!

I remember, I remember
Where it was I used to swing,
And thought the air must rush as fresh
To swallows on the wing;
My spirit flew in feathers then
That is so heavy now,
And summer pools could hardly cool
The fever on my brow.

I remember, I remember
The fir trees dark and high;
I used to think their slender tops
Were close against the sky:
It was a childish ignorance,
But now 'tis little joy
To know I'm farther off from Heaven
Than when I was a boy.

Thomas Hood

THE DAYS ARE CLEAR

The days are clear,
  Day after day,
When April's here
  That leads to May,
And June
Must follow soon:
  Stay, June, stay!
If only we could stop the moon
And June!

CHRISTINA ROSETTI

AUTUMN FIRES

In the other gardens
  And all up the vale,
From the autumn bonfires
  See the smoke trail!

Pleasant summer over
  And all the summer flowers,
The red fire blazes,
  The gray smoke towers.

Sing a song of seasons!
  Something bright in all!
Flowers in the summer,
  Fires in the fall!

ROBERT LOUIS STEVENSON

MY SHADOW

I have a little shadow that goes in and out
    with me,
And what can be the use of him is more
    than I can see.
He is very, very like me from the heels up to
    the head;
And I see him jump before me, when I jump
    into my bed.

The funniest thing about him is the way he
    likes to grow—
Not at all like proper children, which is
    always very slow;
For he sometimes shoots up taller
    like an india-rubber ball,
And he sometimes gets so
    little that there's none
    of him at all.

He hasn't got a notion of how children
  ought to play,
And can only make a fool of me in
  every sort of way.
He stays so close beside me, he's a
  coward you can see;
I'd think shame to stick to nursie
  as that shadow sticks to me!

One morning, very early, before the
  sun was up,
I rose and found the shining dew on
  every buttercup;
    But my lazy little shadow, like an
        arrant sleepyhead,
            Had stayed at home behind
                me and was fast
                asleep in bed.

ROBERT LOUIS STEVENSON

FOR WANT OF A NAIL

For want of a nail, the shoe was lost;
For want of the shoe, the horse was lost;
For want of the horse, the rider was lost;
For want of the rider, the battle was lost;
For want of the battle, the kingdom was los
And all from the want of a horseshoe nail.

ANNA MARIA

Anna Maria she sat on the fire;
The fire was too hot, she sat on the pot;
The pot was too round, she sat on the ground;
The ground was too flat, she sat on the cat;
The cat ran away with Maria on her back.

THE HUMBLE-BEE

Two young men out walking stopped by a stream next to an old ruined house. They noticed how the stream turned into a tiny waterfall crossed by narrow blades of grass. They sat by the stream and soon one was fast asleep, and the other sat watching the view.

Suddenly, a tiny creature, the size of a humble-bee, flew out of the sleeper's mouth. It walked over the grass stalks to cross the stream and then disappeared into the ruin through one of the cracks in the wall.

The man watching was shocked. Then, as he went to shake his companion awake, he saw the creature emerge from the ruin, fly across the stream and re-enter the sleeper's mouth.

As he woke, the young man said, "You have just interrupted the most wonderful dream,

and I wish you had not woken me. I was walking through a grassy plain and came to a wide river. There was a bridge made of silver near a great waterfall, so I walked over the bridge to a beautiful stone palace. The palace was bursting with gold and jewels. I looked at all these fine things, and wondered at the wealth of the person who left them there. I was deciding which I would bring away with me, then suddenly you woke me, and I could bring away none of the riches."

THE WIND

Who has seen the wind?
   Neither I nor you;
But when the leaves hang
  trembling
   The wind is passing through.

Who has seen the wind?
   Neither you nor I;
But when the trees bow down
  their heads
   The wind is passing by.

CHRISTINA ROSSETTI

68

HAPPY THOUGHT

The world is so full of a number
   of things,
I'm sure we should all be as
   happy as kings.

ROBERT LOUIS STEVENSON

69

FROM WIBBLETON
TO WOBBLETON

From Wibbleton to Wobbleton
  is fifteen miles,
From Wobbleton to Wibbleton
  is fifteen miles,
From Wibbleton to Wobbleton,
From Wobbleton to Wibbleton,
From Wibbleton to Wobbleton
  is fifteen miles.

70

SEE-SAW, SACRADOWN

See-saw, Sacradown,
Which is the way to London Town?
One foot up and one foot down,
That's the way to London Town.

WAGTAIL AND BABY

A baby watched a ford, whereto
  A wagtail came for drinking;
A blaring bull went wading through,
  The wagtail showed no shrinking.

A stallion splashed his way across,
  The birdie nearly sinking;
He gave his plumes a twitch and toss
  And held his own unblinking.

Next saw the baby round the spot
  A mongrel slowing slinking;
The wagtail gazed, but faltered not
  In dip and sip and prinking.

A perfect gentleman then neared;
  The wagtail, in a winking,
With terror rose and disappeared;
  The baby fell a-thinking.

THOMAS HARDY

SOLOMON GRUNDY

Solomon Grundy,
Born on Monday,
Christened on Tuesday,
Married on Wednesday,
Sick on Thursday,
Worse on Friday,
Died on Saturday,
Buried on Sunday,
That was the end
Of Solomon Grundy.

LIE A-BED

Lie a-bed,
Sleepy head,
Shut up eyes, bo-peep;
Till day-break
Never wake—
Baby, sleep.

CHRISTINA ROSSETTI

OLD KING COLE

Old King Cole
Was a merry old soul,
And a merry old soul was he;
He called for his pipe,
And he called for his bowl,
And he called for his fiddlers three

Every fiddler had a fine fiddle,
And a very fine fiddle had he;
   Twee tweedle dee, tweedle dee,
      went the fiddlers,
   Very merry men are we;
Oh there's none so rare
As can compare
With King Cole and his fiddlers three.

THE SUGAR-PLUM TREE

Have you ever heard of the
    Sugar-Plum Tree?
'Tis a marvel of great renown!
It blooms on the shore of the
    Lollipop sea,
In the garden of Shut-Eye Town.
The fruit that it bears is so
    wondrously sweet
(As those who have tasted it say),
That good little children have
    only to eat
Of that fruit to be happy next day.

When you've got to the tree, you
would have a hard time
To capture the fruit which I sing;
The tree is so tall that no person
could climb
To the boughs where the
sugar-plums swing.
But up in that tree sits a chocolate cat,
And a gingerbread dog prowls below—
And this is the way you contrive
to get at
Those sugar-plums tempting you so:

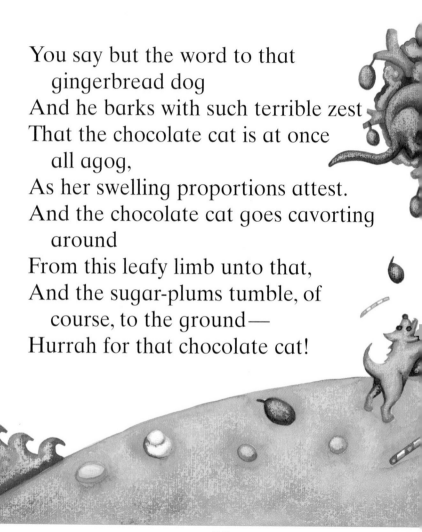

You say but the word to that
  gingerbread dog
And he barks with such terrible zest
That the chocolate cat is at once
  all agog,
As her swelling proportions attest.
And the chocolate cat goes cavorting
  around
From this leafy limb unto that,
And the sugar-plums tumble, of
  course, to the ground—
Hurrah for that chocolate cat!

There are marshmallows, gumdrops,
    and peppermint canes,
With striplings of scarlet or gold,
And you carry away of the treasure
    that rains
As much as your apron can hold!
So come, little child, cuddle closer
    to me
In your dainty white nightcap
    and gown,
And I'll rock you away to that
    Sugar-Plum Tree
    In the garden of Shut-Eye Town.

EUGENE FIELD

THE MAIDEN FROM THE LAKE

A shepherd who lived by the mountains of Caermarthen was watching his sheep near lake one day, when he saw three beautiful maidens rise from the lake. They came to th shore and walked around among the sheep

The shepherd offered one of them some bread. She tried a little, and then said, "You bread's too hard. You won't catch me," and ran back to the lake with the others.

The next day he took some bread that wa: not so well baked. To his delight, they did appear again. But this time the girl said, "Your bread's not baked. You won't catch me." Once more, she returned to the water.

On the third day, when the maidens came, he offered the girl some bread that had bee floating on the water. She liked this bread.

The two talked for a long time before the maiden agreed to marry the shepherd. Before they were married the maiden warned she would be a good wife, unless he struck her three times without reason.

They had three fine sons. They were going to christen one of the boys when the wife said that it was too far to walk to church.

"If you fetch the horses," said the shepherd, "we can ride all the way."

"While I get the horses, will you fetch my gloves from the house?" asked his wife.

When the shepherd returned his wife had not fetched the horses, and he tapped her gently on the shoulder to remind her.

"That's one strike," said his wife.

Another day they were at a wedding when the shepherd found his wife crying. He tapped her on the shoulder as he comforted her.

"Trouble is coming," she replied. "That is the second time you have struck me without reason. Take care to avoid the third time."

One day the couple were at a funeral. The wife laughed loudly. The shepherd could not understand why she laughed, so, touching her rather roughly, he said, "Wife, why are you laughing when all around you are sad?"

"I am laughing because people who die leave their troubles behind them. But your troubles have just begun. You have struck m for a third time. Now I must end our marriage and bid you farewell."

The sad shepherd was surprised when he heard his wife calling all the cattle to follow her to her home below the waters of the lake. The cattle, and a team of oxen with their plow, got up and follow her away. The mark left by the plough can still be seen running across the pastures by the lake. But the lady has only been seen once more. When her sons grew up, she returned to visit them. She gave them miraculous gifts of healing. And ever since, the Doctors of Myddvai have been famous throughout the land of Wales.

HUSH, LITTLE BABY

Hush, little baby, don't say a word,
Papa's going to buy you a mockingbird.

If the mockingbird won't sing,
Papa's going to buy you a diamond ring.

If the diamond ring turns to brass,
Papa's going to buy you a looking-glass.

If the looking-glass gets broke,
Papa's going to buy you a billy-goat.

If that billy-goat runs away,
Papa's going to buy you another today.

ANONYMOUS
AMERICAN

THE MOUSE'S LULLABY

h, rock-a-by, baby mouse, rock-a-by, so!
hen baby's asleep to the baker's I'll go,
nd while he's not looking I'll pop from a hole,
nd bring to my baby a fresh penny roll.

PALMER COX

THE CITY CHILD

Dainty little maiden, whither
    would you wander?
Whither from this pretty home
    the home where mother dwel
"Far and far away," said the
    dainty little maiden,
"All among the gardens,
    auriculas, anemones,
Roses and lilies and
    Canterbury-bells."

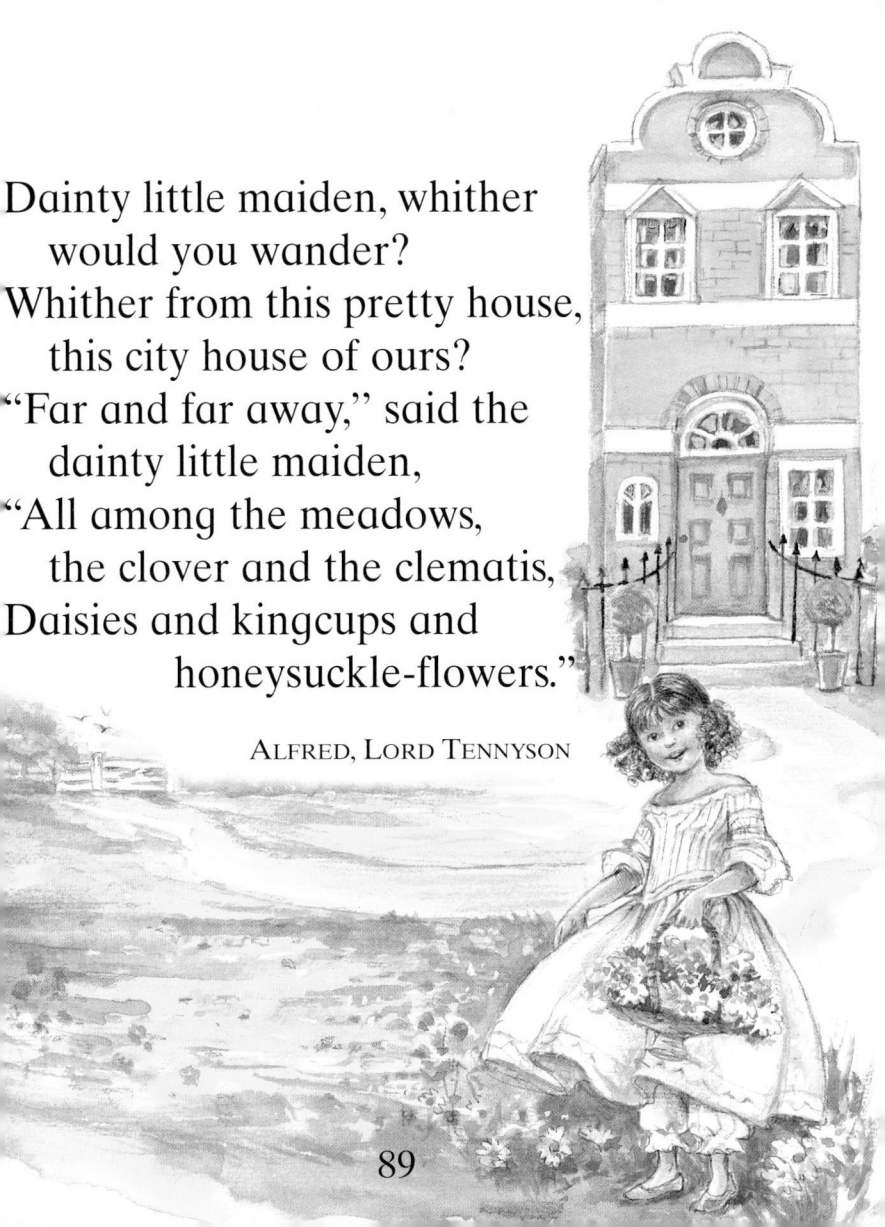

Dainty little maiden, whither
 would you wander?
Whither from this pretty house,
 this city house of ours?
"Far and far away," said the
 dainty little maiden,
"All among the meadows,
 the clover and the clematis,
Daisies and kingcups and
 honeysuckle-flowers."

ALFRED, LORD TENNYSON

I HAD A LITTLE NUT TREE

I had a little nut tree, nothing would it bear,
But a silver nutmeg, and a golden pear;
The King of Spain's daughter came to visit me
And all for the sake of my little nut tree.
I skipped over water, I danced over sea,
And all the birds of the air couldn't catch me.

HOW MANY MILES TO BABYLON?

How many miles to Babylon?
   Threescore and ten.
Can I get there by candlelight?
   Yes, and back again!

THE STORY OF THE LITTLE BIRD

Once long ago in Ireland, a holy man was walking one day in the garden of his monastery, when he decided to pray, to give thanks to God for the beauty of all the flowers, plants, and herbs around him. As he did so, he heard a small bird singing the sweetest song he had ever heard. When the bird flew away from the garden, singing as it went, he followed it.

The bird continued its song in a small grove of trees. As the bird hopped from tree to tree, the monk carried on following, until they had gone a great distance. The more the bird sang, the more the monk was enchanted. The monk realised that it would soon be dark. Reluctantly, he went home, arriving as the sun was going down in the west. As the sun set, the monk thought that the sight was almost as beautiful and heavenly as the song of the little bird he had been listening to. But the glorious sunset was not the only sight that surprised the monk. Everything around him seemed to have changed. Different plants grew in the garden, the brothers had different faces, and even the abbey buildings seemed changed. How could all these changes have taken place in a single afternoon?

The holy man greeted the first monk he saw. "Brother, why has our abbey changed since this morning? There are new plants, new faces, and even the stones of the church seem different."

The second monk looked at him carefully. "Nothing has altered since morning, and you are the only new brother. Although you wear the habit of our order, I have not seen you before." And the two monks looked at each other in wonder. Neither could understand what had happened.

94

The holy man told how he had gone
o walk in the garden and heard the
ird, and how he had followed the creature
nto the countryside to listen to its song.
The second monk looked surprised and
aid, "Our order has a story about a brother
vho went missing two hundred years ago,
fter a bird was heard singing."
The holy man looked at his companion and
eplied, "The time of my death has finally
rrived. Praised be the Lord for his mercies
o me." The holy man died at midnight,
nd was buried in the abbey church.
The monks of the abbey tell the story of
he little bird who was an angel of the Lord.
This was God's way of taking the soul of a
nan who was known for his holiness and
is love of the beauties of nature.

GO TO BED, TOM

Go to bed, Tom,
Go to bed, Tom,
Tired or not, Tom,
Go to bed, Tom.

HIGGLEDY PIGGLEDY

Higgledy piggledy,
Here we lie,
Picked and plucked,
And put in a pie!

WEE WILLIE WINKIE

Wee Willie Winkie runs through the town,
Up-stairs and down-stairs in his nightgown,
Peeping through the keyhole, crying
    through the lock,
"Are the children in their beds, it's past
    eight o'clock?"

PETER, PETER, PUMPKIN EATER

Peter, Peter, pumpkin eater,
Had a wife and couldn't keep her;
He put her in a pumpkin shell
And there he kept her very well.

Peter, Peter, pumpkin eater,
Had another and didn't love her;
Peter learned to read and spell,
And then he loved her very well.

SIMPLE SIMON

Simple Simon met a pieman
　Going to the fair;
Said Simple Simon to the pieman,
　"Let me taste your ware."

Said the pieman to Simple Simon,
　"Show me first your penny";
Said Simple Simon to the pieman,
　"Indeed I have not any."

GIRLS AND BOYS
COME OUT TO PLAY

Girls and boys, come out to play;
The moon doth shine as bright as day;
Leave your supper, and leave your sleep,
And come with your playfellows into the stre
Come with a whoop, come with a call,
Come with a good will or not at all.
Up the ladder and down the wall,
A halfpenny roll will serve us all.
You find milk, and I'll find flour,
And we'll have a pudding in half-an-hour.

GEORGIE PORGIE

Georgie Porgie, pudding and pie,
Kissed the girls and made them cry;
When the boys came out to play
Georgie Porgie ran away.

I SCREAM

I scream, you scream,
We all scream for ice cream!

SNEEZE ON MONDAY

Sneeze on Monday, sneeze for danger
Sneeze on Tuesday, kiss a stranger;
Sneeze on Wednesday, get a letter;
Sneeze on Thursday, something better
Sneeze on Friday, sneeze for sorrow;
Sneeze on Saturday, see your
    sweetheart tomorrow.

SEE A PIN AND PICK IT UP

See a pin and pick it up,
All the day you'll have good luck;
See a pin and let it lay,
Bad luck you'll have all the day!

RAIN, RAIN, GO AWAY

Rain, rain, go away,
Come again
another day.

THE SWING

How do you like to
go up in a swing,
Up in the air
so blue?

Oh, I do think it the
pleasantest thing
Ever a child
can do!

Up in the air and over the wall,
  Till I can see so wide,
Rivers and trees and cattle and all
  Over the countryside—

Till I look down on the garden green,
  Down on the roof so brown—
Up in the air I go flying again,
  Up in the air and down!

ROBERT LOUIS STEVENSON

THREE WISE
MEN OF GOTHAM

Three wise men of Gotham
Went to sea in a bowl:
And if the bowl had been stronger,
My song would have been longer.

JACKANORY

I'll tell you a story
 Of Jackanory,
And now my story's begun;
 I'll tell you another
 Of Jack his brother,
And now my story's done.

ONCE I SAW A LITTLE BIRD

Once I saw a little bird
Come hop, hop, hop;
So I cried, "Little bird,
Will you stop, stop, stop?"
And was going to the window,
To say, "How do you do?"
But he shook his little tail,
And far away he flew.

JAY-BIRD

Jay-bird, jay-bird, settin' on a rail,
Pickin' his teeth with the end
   of his tail;
Mulberry leaves and calico sleeves—
All school teachers are hard to please.

ROBIN AND RICHARD

Robin and Richard were two pretty men;
They laid in bed till the clock struck ten;
Then up starts Robin and looks at the sky,
Oh! brother Richard, the sun's very high:

The bull's in the barn threshing the corn,
The cock's on the dunghill blowing his horn
The cat's at the fire frying of fish,
The dog's in the pantry breaking his dish.

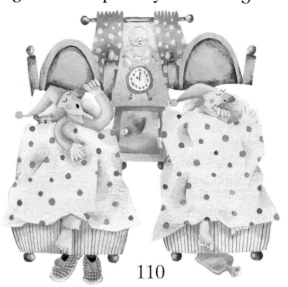

110

LITTLE TOMMY TITTLEMOUSE

Little Tommy Tittlemouse
Lived in a little house;
He caught fishes
In other men's ditches.

SEE-SAW, MARGERY DAW

See-saw, Margery Daw,
  Jack shall have a new master;
He shall have but a penny a day,
  Because he can't work any faster.

HURT NO
LIVING THING

Hurt no living thing,
 Ladybird nor butterfly,
Nor moth with dusty wing,
Nor cricket chirping cheerily,
Nor grasshopper, so light of leap,
 Nor dancing gnat,
 Nor beetle fat,
Nor harmless worms that creep.

CHRISTINA ROSSETTI

THE COW

The friendly cow all red and white,
  I love with all my heart:
She gives me cream with all her might,
  To eat with apple-tart.

She wanders lowing here and there,
  And yet she cannot stray,
All in the pleasant open air,
  The pleasant light of day.

And blown by all the winds that pass
  And wet with all the showers,
She walks among the meadow grass
  And eats the meadow flowers.

ROBERT LOUIS STEVENSON

HUSH-A-BYE, BABY

Hush-a-bye, baby, on the tree top,
When the wind blows the cradle
    will rock;
When the bough breaks the
    cradle will fall,
Down will come baby, cradle
    and all.

ALL THE PRETTY LITTLE HORSES

Hush-a-bye, don't you cry,
Go to sleepy little baby.
When you wake
You shall have
All the pretty little horses.
Blacks and bays,
Dapples and grays,
Coach and six white horses.

Hush-a-bye, don't you cry,
Go to sleepy little baby.
When you wake
You shall have cake
And all the pretty little horses.

LEG OVER LEG

Leg over leg,
   As the dog went to Dover;
   When he came to a stile,
   Jump he went over.

MICHAEL FINNEGAN

There was an old man called
   Michael Finnegan,
He grew whiskers on his chinnegan,
The wind came out and blew
   them in again,
Poor old Michael Finnegan.
   Begin again…

RIDE A COCK-HORSE

Ride a cock-horse to Banbury Cross,
    To see a fine lady ride on a white horse,
Rings on her fingers and bells on her toes,
    She shall have music wherever she goes.

I AM A GOLD LOCK

FOR TWO VOICES

I am a gold lock.
I am a gold key.
I am a silver lock.
I am a silver key.
I am a brass lock.
I am a brass key.
I am a lead lock.
I am a lead key.
I am a monk lock.
I am a monk key!

I WENT UP ONE PAIR OF STAIRS

FOR TWO VOICES

I went up one pair of stairs.
  Just like me.
I went up two pair of stairs.
  Just like me.
I went into a room.
  Just like me.
I looked out of a window.
  Just like me.
And there I saw a monkey.
  Just like me.

UNCLE JOHN IS VERY SICK

Uncle John is very sick, what shall we
    send him?
A piece of pie, a piece of cake, a piece
    of apple dumpling.
What shall we send it in? In a piece of paper
Paper is not fine enough; in a golden saucer.
Who shall we send it by? By the
    governor's daughter.
Take her by the lily-white hand, and
    lead her over the water.

THE GRAND OLD DUKE OF YORK

The grand old Duke of York,
  He had ten thousand men;
He marched them up to the top
 of the hill,
    And he marched them down again!
And when they were up they were up,
    And when they were down they
     were down;
And when they were only halfway up,
  They were neither up nor down.

THE KANGAROO

Old Jumpety-Bumpety-Hop-and-Go-One
Was lying asleep on his side in the sun.
This old kangaroo, he was whisking the flies
(With his long glossy tail) from his ears
   and his eyes.
Jumpety-Bumpety-Hop-and-Go-One
Was lying asleep on his side in the sun,
Jumpety-Bumpety-Hop!

ANONYMOUS
AUSTRALIAN

122

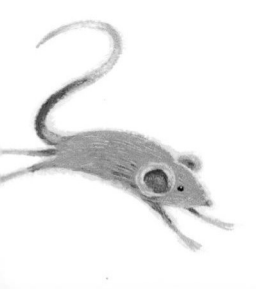

THE EAGLE

He clasps the crag with crooked hands;
Close to the sun in lonely lands,
Ring'd with the azure world, he stands.

The wrinkled sea beneath him crawls;
He watches from his mountain walls,
And like a thunderbolt he falls.

ALFRED, LORD TENNYSON

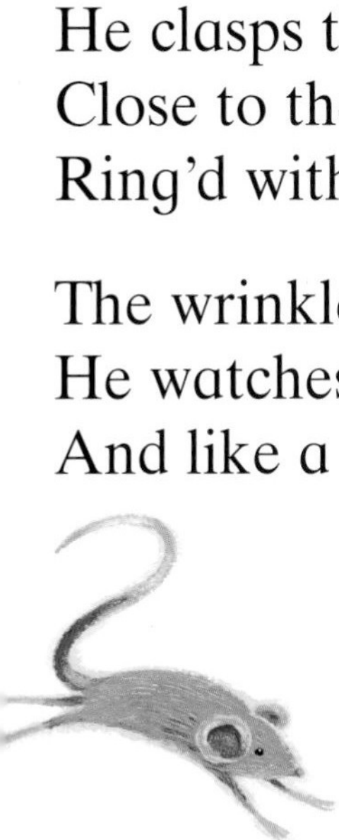

123

SKILLYWIDDEN

A man was cutting furze on Trendreen Hill when he saw one of the little people, fast asleep, on the heath. The man took off the cuff that he wore at his work, and popped the little man in before he could wake up. Then he carried his find home, and let the creature out on to the hearth stone.

The family called him Bob of the Heath, and Bob told the man he would show him where to find gold hidden on the hillside.

Several days later, after the furze harvest, the neighbors came to the man's house to celebrate. To hide Bob, the man locked him in the barn with the children.

But the fairy and his playmates soon found a way out. Before long they were playing a game of dancing and hide-and-seek all round the great heap of furze in the yard. Suddenly they saw a tiny man and woman marching round the furze. "Oh my poor Skillywidden," said the woman. "Where can you be? Will I ever set eyes on you again?" "Go back indoors," said Bob to the children. "My mother and father have come looking for me." Then he cried, "Here I am mommy!" And with that, Bob vanished with his parents, leaving the children in the yard.

When they told their father what had happened, the man was angry, and gave them a beating for escaping from the locked barn. After this the man sometimes went to Trendreen Hill to look for fairies and crocks of gold. But he was never able to find either.

WINTER

When icicles hang by the wall,
  And Dick the shepherd blows his nail,
And Tom bears logs into the hall,
  And milk comes frozen home in pail;
When blood is nipp'd and ways be foul,
Then nightly sings the staring owl,
    To-whit! to-who!
    A merry note,
While greasy Joan doth keel the pot.

When all aloud the wind doth blow,
  And coughing drowns the parson's saw;
And birds sit brooding in the snow,
  And Marian's nose looks red and raw;
When roasted crabs hiss in the bowl,
Then nightly sings the staring owl,
  To-whit! to-who!
  A merry note,
While greasy Joan doth keel the pot.

WILLIAM SHAKESPEARE

JACK AND GUY

Jack and Guy
Went out in the rye,
And they found a little boy
   with one black eye.
Come, says Jack, let's knock
   him on the head.
No, says Guy, let's buy him
   some bread;

You buy one loaf and I'll
   buy two,
And we'll bring him up as
   other folk do.

FIRE ON THE MOUNTAIN

Rats in the garden—catch'em Towser!
Cows in the cornfield—run boys run!
Cat's in the cream pot—stop her now, sir!
Fire on the mountain—run boys run!

BILLY BOOSTER

Billy Billy Booster,
Had a little rooster,
The rooster died
And Billy cried.
Poor Billy Booster.

JACK, JACK, THE BREAD'S A-BURNING

Jack, Jack, the bread's a-burning,
All to a cinder;
If you don't come and fetch it out
We'll throw it through the window.

JACK AND JILL

Jack and Jill went up the hill
 To fetch a pail of water;
Jack fell down and broke his crown,
 And Jill came tumbling after.

Up Jack got, and home did trot,
 As fast as he could caper,
He went to bed to mend his head
 With vinegar and brown paper.

TOMMY SNOOKS AND BESSY

As Tommy Snooks and Bessy Brooks
Were walking out one Sunday,
Says Tommy Snooks to Bessy Brooks,
"Tomorrow will be Monday."

LITTLE JUMPING JOAN

Here am I, little jumping Joan.
When nobody's with me,
I'm always alone.

THERE WAS A LITTLE GIRL

There was a little girl, and she had
    a little curl
Right in the middle of her forehead;
When she was good she was very,
    very good,
But when she was bad she was horrid.

BLACK LAD MacCRIMMON

A young man called Black Lad MacCrimmo
was the most down-trodden of three brother
His brothers were always given more food,
and allowed more enjoyment than Black La
and he was always given the hardest jobs to
do when they were working together.

The father and the elder brothers had a fin
set of pipes that they liked to play. Black La
would have liked to have played the pipes,
but the brothers took up too much time witl
their playing to give the young lad a chance

People said that the greatest musicians of a
were the fairy folk. Black Lad hoped that or
day he would meet one of the little people s
they could teach him to master the pipes.

One day the lad's father and his brothers
were getting ready to go to the fair. Black Lo

wanted to go, but they would not take him. So he took up the chanter from the set of pipes to see if he could play a tune. He was so absorbed in what he was doing, he did not see someone watching him and listening.

Suddenly a voice spoke in his ear: "You are doing well with your music, lad." It was none other than the Banshee from the castle.

"Which do you prefer," continued the Banshee. "Skill without success or success without skill?"

The lad replied that most of ɑ
he wanted skill, he did not caɪ
about success. The Banshee
smiled, and pulled a hair froɪ
her head which she wound
around the reed of the chantɾ
Turning to Black Lad she saiɗ
"Put your fingers on the holes of
the chanter, and I will place my fingers oveɪ
yours to guide you. Think of a tune to play,
and my skill will rub off on you."

Soon the lad played with great skill, and
could master any tune that he thought of.

"Indeed you are the King of the Pipers,"
said the Banshee. "There has been none
better before you, and none better shall
come after." And with this blessing, the
Banshee went on her way back to the castlɾ

BLACK LAD MacCRIMMON

Black Lad found he could play
any tune. As his father and
brothers returned, they could
hear him playing, but by the
time they entered the house,
the lad had put away the pipes,
as if nothing at all had happened.
The lad's father took down the pipes,
and he and his first and second sons played. But,
instead of putting the pipes away, the father
gave them to the lad, saying, "You shall no
longer spend all day doing the hardest of the
work and eating the meanest of the food."
They heard that Black Lad was far better than
any of them. "There is no longer any point in
our playing," said the father to the two eldest
sons. "The lad is truly King of the Pipers."
And the lad's brothers knew it was true.

TIGGY-TOUCHWOOD

Tiggy-tiggy-touchwood, my black hen,
She lays eggs for gentlemen,
Sometimes nine and sometimes ten,
Tiggy-tiggy-touchwood, my black hen.

MRS. HEN

Chook, chook, chook, chook, chook,
  Good morning, Mrs. Hen.
How many chickens have you got?
  Madam, I've got ten.

Four of them are yellow,
  And four of them are brown,
And two of them are speckled red,
  The nicest in the town.

THE WISE OLD OWL

There was an old owl who lived in an oak.
The more he heard, the less he spoke.
The less he spoke, the more he heard,
Why aren't we like that wise old bird!

THERE WAS AN OLD CROW

There was an old crow
  Sat upon a clod,
There's an end of my song,
  That's odd!

HARK THE ROBBERS

Hark at the robbers going through,
  Through, through, through; through,
  through, through;
Hark at the robbers going through,
  My fair lady.

What have the robbers done to you,
  You, you, you; you, you, you?
What have the robbers done to you,
  My fair lady?

Stole my gold watch and chain,
  Chain, chain, chain; chain, chain,
    chain;
Stole my gold watch and chain,
  My fair lady.

How many dollars will set us free,
  Free, free, free; free, free, free?
How many dollars will set us free,
  My fair lady?

A hundred dollars
   will set you free,
    Free, free, free; free, free, free;
A hundred dollars will set you free,
   My fair lady.

We have not a hundred dollars,
   A hundred dollars;
    a hundred dollars ;
We have not a hundred dollars,
   My fair lady.

Then to prison you must go,
  Go, go, go; go, go, go;
Then to prison you must go,
  My fair lady.

To prison we will not go,
  Go, go, go; go, go, go;
To prison we will not go,
  My fair lady.

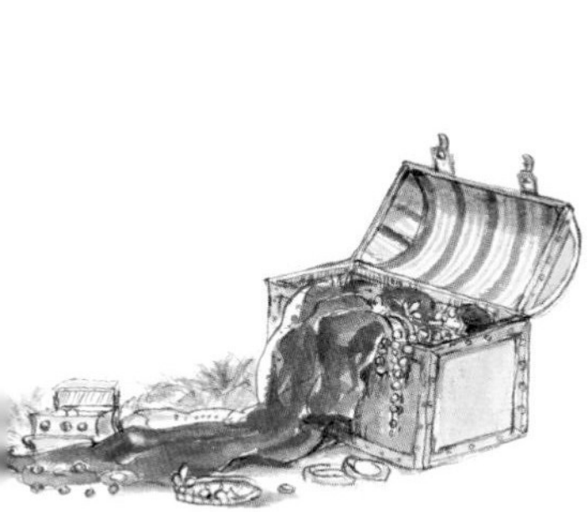

145

IN THE TREE-TOP

"Rock-a-by, baby, up in
   the tree-top!"
Mother his blanket
   is spinning;
And a light little rustle
   that never will stop,
Breezes and boughs
   are beginning.
Rock-a-by, baby,
   swinging so high!
          Rock-a-by!

"When the wind blows, then the
    cradle will rock."
Hush! now it stirs in the bushes;
Now with a whisper, a flutter of talk,
Baby and hammock it pushes.
Rock-a-by, baby! shut, pretty eye!
                      Rock-a-by!

"Rock with the boughs, rock-a-by,
    baby dear!"
Leaf-tongues are singing and saying;
Mother she listens, and sister is near,
Under the tree softly playing.
Rock-a-by, baby! mother's close by!
                    Rock-a-by!

Weave him a beautiful dream,
  little breeze!
Little leaves, nestle around him!
He will remember the song of the trees,
When age with silver has crowned him.
Rock-a-by, baby! wake by-and-by!
                              Rock-a-by!

Lucy Larcom

TWO LITTLE KITTENS

Two little kittens
One stormy night,
Began to quarrel,
And then to fight.

One had a mouse
And the other had none;
And that was the way
The quarrel begun.

"I'll have that mouse,"
Said the bigger cat.
"You'll have that mouse?
We'll see about that!"

"I will have that mouse,"
Said the tortoise-shell;
And, spitting and scratching,
On her sister she fell.

I've told you before
'Twas a stormy night,
When these two kittens
Began to fight.

The old woman took
The sweeping broom,
And swept them both
Right out of the room.

The ground was covered
With frost and snow,
They had lost the mouse,
And had nowhere to go.

So they lay and shivered
Beside the door,
Till the old woman finished
Sweeping the floor.

And then they crept in
As quiet as mice,
All wet with snow
And as cold as ice.

They found it much better
That stormy night,
To lie by the fire,
Than to quarrel and fight.

JANE TAYLOR

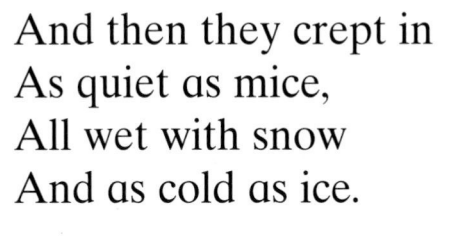

LITTLE JACK HORNER

Little Jack Horner
Sat in a corner,
Eating his Christmas pie;
He put in his thumb,
And pulled out a plum,
And said: "What a good boy am I!"

WHEN JACKY'S A VERY GOOD BOY

When Jacky's a very good boy,
He shall have cakes and a custard;
But when he does nothing but cry,
He shall have nothing but mustard.

LITTLE TOMMY TUCKER

Little Tommy Tucker
  Sings for his supper:
What shall we give him?
  Brown bread and butter.
How shall he cut it
  Without a knife?
How can he marry
  Without a wife?

GOING DOWN HILL ON A BICYCLE

With lifted feet, hands still,
I am poised, and down the hill
Dart, with heedful mind;
The air goes by in a wind.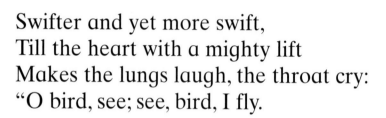

Swifter and yet more swift,
Till the heart with a mighty lift
Makes the lungs laugh, the throat cry:
"O bird, see; see, bird, I fly.

"Is this, is this your joy?
O bird, then I, though a boy,
For a golden moment share
Your feathery life in air!"

Say, heart, is there aught like this
In a world that is full of bliss?
'Tis more than skating, bound
Steel-shod to the level ground.

Speed slackens now, I float
Awhile in my airy boat;
Till, when the wheels scarce crawl,
My feet to the treadles fall.

Alas, that the longest hill
Must end in a vale; but still,
Who climbs with toil, wheresoe'er,
Shall find wings waiting there.

HENRY CHARLES BEECHING

MEG MERRILEES

Old Meg she was a Gipsy,
  And lived upon the moors:
Her bed it was the brown heath turf,
  And her house was out of doors.

Her apples were swart blackberries,
  Her currants pods o'broom;
Her wine was dew of the wild white rose,
  Her book a churchyard tomb.

Her Brothers were the craggy hills,
  Her Sisters larchen trees;
Alone with her great family
  She lived as she did please.

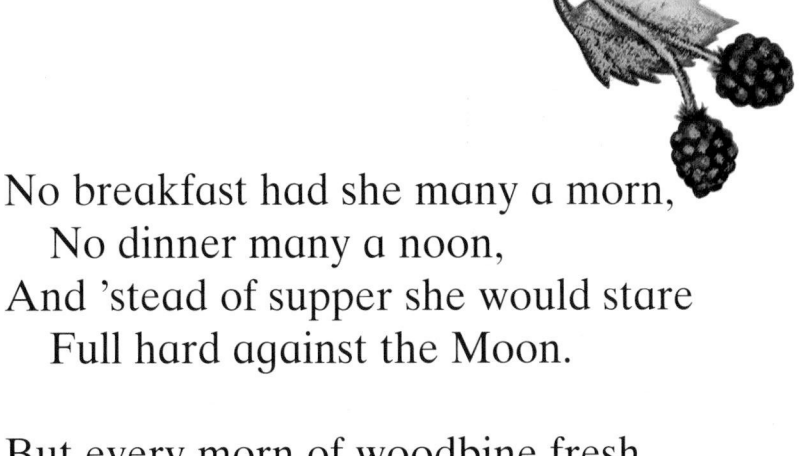

No breakfast had she many a morn,
   No dinner many a noon,
And 'stead of supper she would stare
   Full hard against the Moon.

But every morn of woodbine fresh
   She made her garlanding,
And every night the dark glen Yew
   She wove, and she would sing.

And with her fingers, old and brown,
   She plaited Mats o' Rushes,
And gave them to the Cottagers
   She met among the Bushes.

Old Meg was brave as Margaret Queen,
   And tall as Amazon;
An old red blanket cloak she wore;
   A chip hat had she on.
God rest her aged bones somewhere—
   She died full long agone!

JOHN KEATS

OLD JOE BROWN

Old Joe Brown, he had a wife,
  She was all of eight feet tall.
She slept with her head in the kitchen,
  And her feet stuck out in the hall.

THE MONTHS

Thirty days has September,
April, June, and November;
All the rest have thirty-one,
Excepting February alone,
And that has twenty-eight days clear
And twenty-nine in each leap year.

ROBERT ROWLEY

Robert Rowley rolled a round roll round,
A round roll Robert Rowley rolled round;
Where rolled the round roll Robert
Rowley rolled round?

DANDY

I had a dog and his name
　　was Dandy,
His tail was long and his legs
　　were bandy,
His eyes were brown and
　　his coat was sandy,
The best in the world was
　　my dog Dandy!

FUZZY WUZZY

uzzy Wuzzy was a bear,
　A bear was Fuzzy Wuzzy.
/hen Fuzzy Wuzzy lost his hair
　He wasn't fuzzy, was he?

ONE MISTY MOISTY MORNING

One misty moisty morning,
When cloudy was the weather,
There I met an old man
Clothed all in leather;

Clothed all in leather,
With cap under his chin—
How do you do, and how do
    you do,
And how do you do again!

THERE WAS A CROOKED MAN

There was a crooked man, and he
    went a crooked mile,
He found a crooked sixpence against
    a crooked stile;
He bought a crooked cat, which
    caught a crooked mouse,
And they all lived together in a little
    crooked house.

ROBIN THE BOBBIN

Robin the Bobbin, the big-bellied Ben,
He ate more meat than fourscore men;
He ate a cow, he ate a calf,
He ate a butcher and a half;
He ate a church, he ate a steeple,
He ate the priest and all the people!

    A cow and a calf,
    An ox and a half,
    A church and a steeple,
    And all the good people,
And yet he complained that his
  stomach wasn't full.

HECTOR PROTECTOR

Hector Protector was dressed all in green;
Hector Protector was sent to the Queen.
The Queen did not like him,
Nor more did the King;
So Hector Protector was sent back again.

WASH, HANDS, WASH

Wash, hands, wash,
   Daddy's gone to plow;
If you want your hands washed,
   Have them washed now.

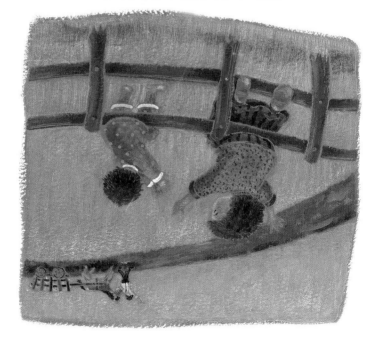

CLAP HANDS

Clap hands for Daddy coming
Down the wagon way,
With a pocketful of money
And a cartload of hay.

COME TO BED, SAYS
SLEEPY-HEAD

"Come to bed,"
Says Sleepy-head;
   "Tarry a while," says Slow;
"Put on the pot,"
Says Greedy-gut,
   "Let's sup before we go."

DIDDLE, DIDDLE, DUMPLING

Diddle, diddle, dumpling, my son John
Went to bed with his trousers on;
One shoe off, the other shoe on,
Diddle, diddle, dumpling, my son John.

FOR EVERY EVIL UNDER THE SU

For every evil under the sun,
There is a remedy, or there is none.
If there be one, try and find it;
If there be none, never mind it.

SALLY GO ROUND THE MOON

Sally go round the moon,
Sally go round the stars;
Sally go round the moon
On a Sunday afternoon.

EPIGRAM

*Engraved on the Collar of a Dog which
I Gave to His Royal Highness*

I am his Highness' Dog at Kew:
Pray tell me, sir, whose dog are you?

ALEXANDER POPE

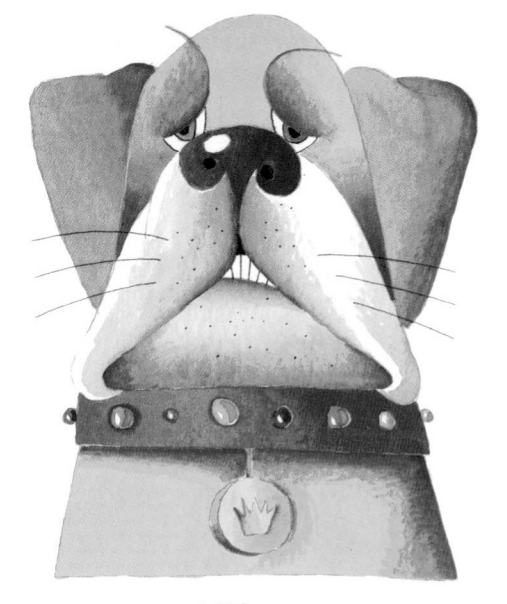

BOW, WOW, WOW

Bow, wow, wow,
  Whose dog art thou?
"Little Tom Tinker's dog,
  Bow, wow, wow."

TWO LITTLE DOGS

Two little dogs
Sat by the fire
Over a fender of coal-dust;
Said one little dog
To the other little dog,
If you don't talk, why, I must.

PUSSY-CAT SITS BY THE FIRE

Pussy-cat sits by the fire.
  How did she come there?
In walks the little dog,
  Says, "Pussy! are you there?
How do you do, Mistress Pussy?
  Mistress Pussy, how d'ye do?"
"I thank you kindly, little dog,
  I fare as well as you!"

INTERY, MINTERY, CUTERY, CORN

Intery, mintery, cutery, corn,
Apple seed and apple thorn.
Wire, briar, limber, lock,
Three geese in a flock.
One flew east and one flew west;
One flew over the cuckoo's nest.

THE CUCKOO

Cuckoo, Cuckoo,
What do you do?
In April
I open my bill;
In May
I sing night and day;
In June
I change my tune;
In July
Away I fly;
In August
Away I must.

THE LOST KINGDOM

In former times, the fertile plains and lush grasslands of West Wales made fine farming country. But it was often flooded by the sea. So the kings of the West built a great wall, with strong sluice gates, to hold back the sea. The people enjoyed a life without floods and they became the envy of all Wales.

One of the greatest of all the western kings was Gwyddno. Sixteen beautiful cities grew up in his kingdom while he reigned, and the lands of the West became even more prosperous.

After the king, the most important person was Seithennin, keeper of the sluices. When a storm brewed, he would close the great sluice gates, and the land would be safe.

But there was a problem. Seithennin was a drunkard. Sometimes he would be late to close the gates, and there would be some slight flooding. But the kingdom would recover, and no great harm was done.

One day, King Gwyddno ordered a great banquet in his hall. All the lords and ladies of the kingdom were there, as well as other men of importance such as Seithennin, and the banquet went on long into the night.

179

Everyone was enjoying themselves, but because of all the noise, no-one could hear the great storm brewing up outside. When people did start to notice, they assumed that Seithennin had closed the sluice gates. But he had drunk more than anyone else at the banquet and was fast asleep.

The fields flooded and the streets were awash. But the banquet went on, until the flood waters poured through the doors of Gwyddno's hall.

There had been floods before the sea wall was built. But this time it was worse. The water was unstoppable. Men, women, and children, lords and servants alike, were swept under the flood. Sheep and cattle went the same way. Soon the whole great kingdom of the West was deep under the water. All were

drowned apart from the poet Taliesin, who survived to tell the tale.

The sea now covers Gwyddno's kingdom, in the place now called Cardigan Bay. Sailors and fishermen who cross the bay say that they can sometimes hear the bells of the sixteen cities, sounding beneath the waves, reminding them of the terrible power of the sea. Some even say that on a quiet, still day they can hear the echoing sound of Gwyddno's final sigh.

HERE COMES A WIDOW

Here comes a widow from Barbary-land
With all her children in her hand;
One can brew, and one can bake,
And one can make a wedding-cake.
  Pray take one,
  Pray take two,
Pray take one that pleases you.

MISS MARY MACK

Miss Mary Mack, Mack, Mack,
All dressed in black, black, black,
With silver buttons, buttons, buttons,
All down her back, back, back.
She went upstairs to make her bed,
She made a mistake and bumped her head;
She went downstairs to wash the dishes,
She made a mistake and washed her wishes;
She went outside to hang her clothes,
She made a mistake and hung her nose.

THERE WAS AN OLD MAN WITH A BEARD

There was an old Man with a beard,
Who said, "It is just as I feared!—
Two Owls and a Hen, four Larks and a Wre
Have all built their nests in my beard!"

EDWARD LE

THERE WAS AN OLD MAN FROM PERU

There was an old man from Peru
Who dreamed he was eating his shoe,
He woke in a fright
In the middle of the night
And found it was perfectly true.

ANONYMOUS
ENGLISH

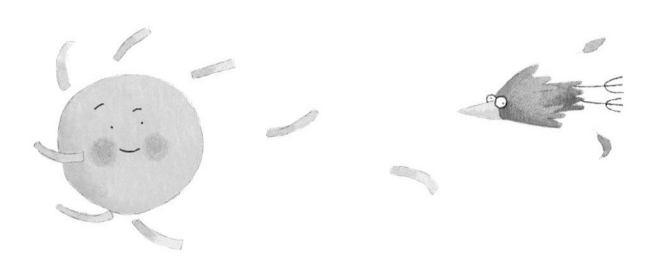

LITTLE WIND

Little wind blow on the hill-top;
Little wind, blow down the plain;
Little wind, blow up the sunshine,
Little wind, blow off the rain.

KATE GREENAWAY

LITTLE BOY BLUE

Little Boy Blue,
  Come blow your horn,
The sheep's in the meadow,
  The cow's in the corn.

Where is the boy
  Who looks after the sheep?
He's under a haycock
  Fast asleep.
Will you wake him?
  No, not I,
For if I do,
  He's sure to cry.

THERE WAS A LITTLE BOY

There was a little boy went into a barn,
  And lay down on some hay;
An owl came out and flew about,
  And the little boy ran away.

ELSIE MARLEY

Elsie Marley is grown so fine,
   She won't get up to serve the swine,
But lies in bed till eight or nine,
   And surely she does take her time.

MARY, MARY

Mary, Mary, quite contrary,
How does your garden grow?
With silver bells, and cockle shells,
And pretty maids all in a row.

ROCK-A-BYE, BABY

Rock-a-bye, baby, thy cradle is green;
Father's a nobleman, Mother's a queen,
And Betty's a lady, and wears a gold ring,
And Johnny's a drummer, and drums
   for the King.

BYE, BABY BUNTING

Bye, baby bunting,
Father's gone a-hunting,
To fetch a little rabbit-skin
To wrap his baby bunting in.

CATERPILLAR

Brown and furry
Caterpillar in a hurry,
Take your walk
To the shady leaf, or stalk,
Or what not,
Which may be the chosen spot.
No toad spy you,
Hovering bird of prey pass by you;
Spin and die,
To live again a butterfly.

CHRISTINA ROSSETTI

THE MAN IN THE MOON

The man in the moon,
 Came tumbling down,
And asked his way to Norwich.
 He went by the south,
 And burnt his mouth
With supping cold pease-porridge.

HANDY SPANDY, JACK-A-DANDY

Handy Spandy, Jack-a-dandy
Loved plum-cake and sugar-candy;
He bought some at a grocer's shop,
And out he came, hop, hop, hop.

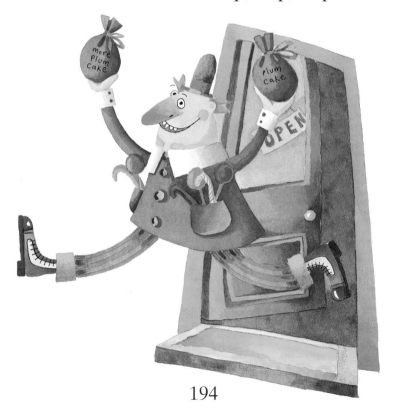

PEASE-PUDDING HOT

Pease-pudding hot,
  Pease-pudding cold,
Pease-pudding in the pot,
  Nine days old.
Some like it hot,
  Some like it cold,
Some like it in the pot,
  Nine days old.

JEREMIAH

Jeremiah
Jumped in the fire.
Fire was so hot
He jumped in the pot.
Pot was so little
He jumped in the kettle.
Kettle was so black
He jumped in the crack.
Crack was so high
He jumped in the sky.
Sky was so blue
He jumped in a canoe.

Canoe was so deep
He jumped in the creek.
Creek was so shallow
He jumped in the tallow.
Tallow was so soft
He jumped in the loft.
Loft was so rotten
He jumped in the cotton.
Cotton was so white
He jumped all night.

HAVE YOU SEEN THE MUFFIN MAN?

Have you seen the muffin man, the
  muffin man, the muffin man,
Have you seen the muffin man that
  lives in Drury Lane O?
Yes, I've seen the muffin man, the
  muffin man, the muffin man;
Yes, I've seen the muffin man who
  lives in Drury Lane O.

LITTLE SALLY WATERS

Little Sally Waters,
Sitting in the sun,
Crying and weeping,
For a young man.
Rise, Sally, rise,
Dry your weeping eyes,
Fly to the east,
Fly to the west,
Fly to the one you love the best.

MAGPIES

One for sorrow, two for joy,
Three for a girl, four for a boy,
Five for silver, six for gold,
Seven for a secret never to be told.

LITTLE ROBIN REDBREAST

Little Robin Redbreast
    Sat upon a rail:
Niddle-noddle went his head
    Wiggle-waggle went his tail!

THE NORTH WIND DOTH BLOW

The north wind doth blow,
And we shall have snow,
And what will poor Robin do then?
                    Poor thing!

He'll sit in a barn,
To keep himself warm,
And hide his head under his wing.
                    Poor thing!

THERE WERE TWO BIRDS
SAT ON A STONE

There were two birds sat on a stone,
    Fa, la, la, la, lal, de;
One flew away, then there was one,
    Fa, la, la, la, lal, de;
The other flew after, and then there
        was none,
    Fa, la, la, la, lal, de;
And so the poor stone was left all alone
    Fa, la, la, la, lal, de!

TWO LITTLE DICKY BIRDS

Two little dicky birds sitting on a wall,
One named Peter, one named Paul.
    Fly away, Peter!
    Fly away, Paul!
      Come back, Peter!
      Come back, Paul!

WHOLE DUTY OF CHILDREN

A child should always say what's true,
And speak when he is spoken to,
And behave mannerly at table:
At least as far as he is able.

ROBERT LOUIS STEVENSON

DON'T CARE

Don't care didn't care;
   Don't care was wild.
Don't care stole plum and pear
   Like any beggar's child.

Don't care was made to care,
   Don't care was hung:
Don't care was put in the pot
   And boiled till he was done.

ANONYMOUS
ENGLISH

A RARE QUARRY

Two friends walked beside a stream, looking
at the banks for holes where otters might be
hiding. Suddenly there was a flash of red.
The creature moved quickly, darting along
the bank, and vanished into a hole by a tree.

One friend asked the other: "What was
that? Could it be a rare, red-furred otter?"

They had never seen such an otter before,
so decided to try to catch it. The burrow had
an entrance on either side of the tree, so they
needed a sack. One of the men found one
and held it over one end of the burrow, while
his friend stood at the other end and made a
noise. There was a mighty plop as the
creature jumped into the sack, then, the two
men made off for home, very pleased with
their rare quarry.

As the pair walked home across the fields they were amazed to hear a voice inside the sack calling, "I hear my mother calling. I hear my mother calling." The men dropped the sack and watched as a tiny figure climbed out. He wore pants, jacket, shoes, and a hat that were bright red. As he ran off towards some low bushes, he looked like a streak of red, and the men saw their mistake.

Looking at each other in alarm, the hunters ran off towards home. They never hunted for otters again on that stretch of the river.

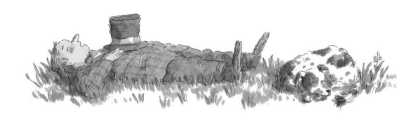

TOMMY TROT

Tommy Trot, a man of law,
Sold his bed and lay upon straw:
Sold the straw and slept on grass,
To buy his wife a looking-glass.

TUMBLING

In jumping and tumbling
  We spend the whole day,
Till night by arriving
  Has finished our play.

What then? One and all,
  There's no more to be said,
As we tumbled all day,
  So we tumble to bed.

BOBBIE SHAFTOE'S GONE TO SEA

Bobbie Shaftoe's gone to sea,
Silver buckles at his knee;
When he comes back he'll marry me,
Bonny Bobbie Shaftoe!

JOHNNY SHALL HAVE A NEW BONNET

Johnny shall have a new bonnet,
  And Johnny shall go to the fair,
And Johnny shall have a blue ribbon
  To tie up his bonny brown hair.

AGAINST QUARRELING AND FIGHTING

Let dogs delight to bark and bite,
  For God hath made them so:
Let bears and lions growl and fight,
  For 'tis their nature, too.

But, children, you should never let
  Such angry passions rise:
Your little hands were never made
  To tear each other's eyes.

Let love through all your actions run,
 And all your words be mild:
Live like the blessed Virgin's Son,
 That sweet and lovely child.

His soul was gentle as a lamb;
 And as his nature grew,
He grew in favor both with man,
 And God his Father, too.

Now, Lord of all, he reigns above,
 And from his heavenly throne
He sees what children dwell in love,
 And marks them for his own.

ISAAC WATTS

THE SPRIGHTLY TAILOR

Long ago, a laird called the great MacDonald lived in a castle called Sandell. MacDonald's favorite garments were called trews, a combination of undershirt and pants in one piece. One day the laird needed some new trews, and called for the local tailor.

MacDonald told the tailor what he wanted. "I'll pay you extra if you will make the trews in the church by night," promised the laird.

MacDonald thought that a fearful monster haunted the church, and he wanted to see how the tailor coped with the beast.

The tailor had heard stories about the monster, but he was tempted by the extra money. So that very night he

walked to the dark church, sat
on a tombstone and sewed.

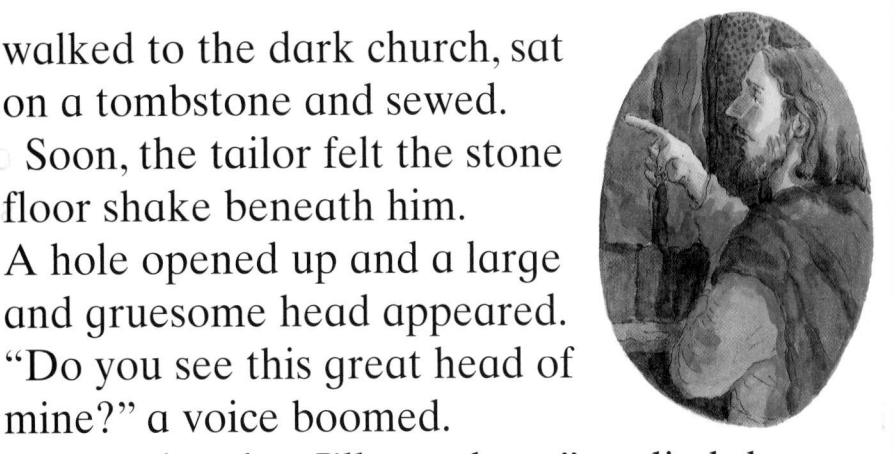

Soon, the tailor felt the stone
floor shake beneath him.
A hole opened up and a large
and gruesome head appeared.
"Do you see this great head of
mine?" a voice boomed.

"I see that, but I'll sew these," replied the
tailor, holding up the trews.

The head rose higher, revealing a thick,
muscular neck. "Do you see this great neck
of mine?" the monster asked.

"I see that, but I'll sew these," said the tailor.

Then the shoulders and trunk came into
view. "Do you see this great chest of mine?"

"I see that, but I'll sew these," said the tailor
as he carried on sewing, although to tell the
truth, some of the stitches were not too neat.

Now the great voice echoed around: "Do you see these great arms of mine?"

"I see those, but I'll sew these," replied the tailor. He carried on with his work, for he wanted to finish by daybreak and claim his payment from the great MacDonald.

The monster gave a great grunt and lifted his first leg out of the ground. "Do you see this great leg of mine?" he asked.

"I see that, but I'll sew these," replied the tailor, and made his stitches a little longer, so that he could finish the trews before the monster could climb right out of his hole.

As the creature began to climb out, the tailor blew out his candle and bundled his things under one arm. Heavy footsteps echoed on the stone floor as the tailor ran out.

The tailor ran for his life. The monster roared at him to stop, but the tailor hurried on until the great castle loomed ahead.

Quickly the gates closed behind the tailor. Just as the great wooden gates slammed shut, the monster crashed into the wall.

To this day, the monster's handprint can be seen on the wall of the castle at Sandell. MacDonald paid the tailor for his work, and gave him a handsome bonus for braving the haunted church. The laird liked his smart new trews, and never realised that some of the stitches were longer and less neat than the others.

GOLDY LOCKS, GOLDY LOCKS

Goldy locks, goldy locks,
   Wilt thou be mine?
Thou shalt not wash dishes,
   Nor yet feed the swine;

But sit on a cushion,
   And sew a fine seam,
And feed upon strawberries,
   Sugar and cream.

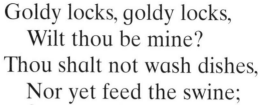

LAVENDER'S BLUE

Lilies are white,
Rosemary's green;
When you are king,
I will be queen.

Roses are red,
Lavender's blue;
If you will have me,
I will have you.

FROM A RAILWAY CARRIAGE

Faster than fairies, faster than witches,
Bridges and houses, hedges and ditches;
And charging along like troops in a
  battle,
All through the meadows, the horses
  and cattle:
All of the sights of the hill and the plain
Fly as thick as driving rain;
And ever again, in the wink of an eye,
Painted stations whistle by.

Here is a child who clambers
     and scrambles,
All by himself and gathering brambles;
Here is a tramp who stands and gazes;
And there is the green for stringing
     the daisies!
Here is a cart run away in the road
Lumping along with man and load;
And here is a mill, and there is a river:
Each a glimpse and gone for ever!

ROBERT LOUIS STEVENSON

THAW

Over the land freckled
   with snow half-thawed
The speculating rooks at
   their nests cawed
And saw from elm-tops,
   delicate as flower of grass,
What we below could
   not see, winter pass.

EDWARD THOMAS